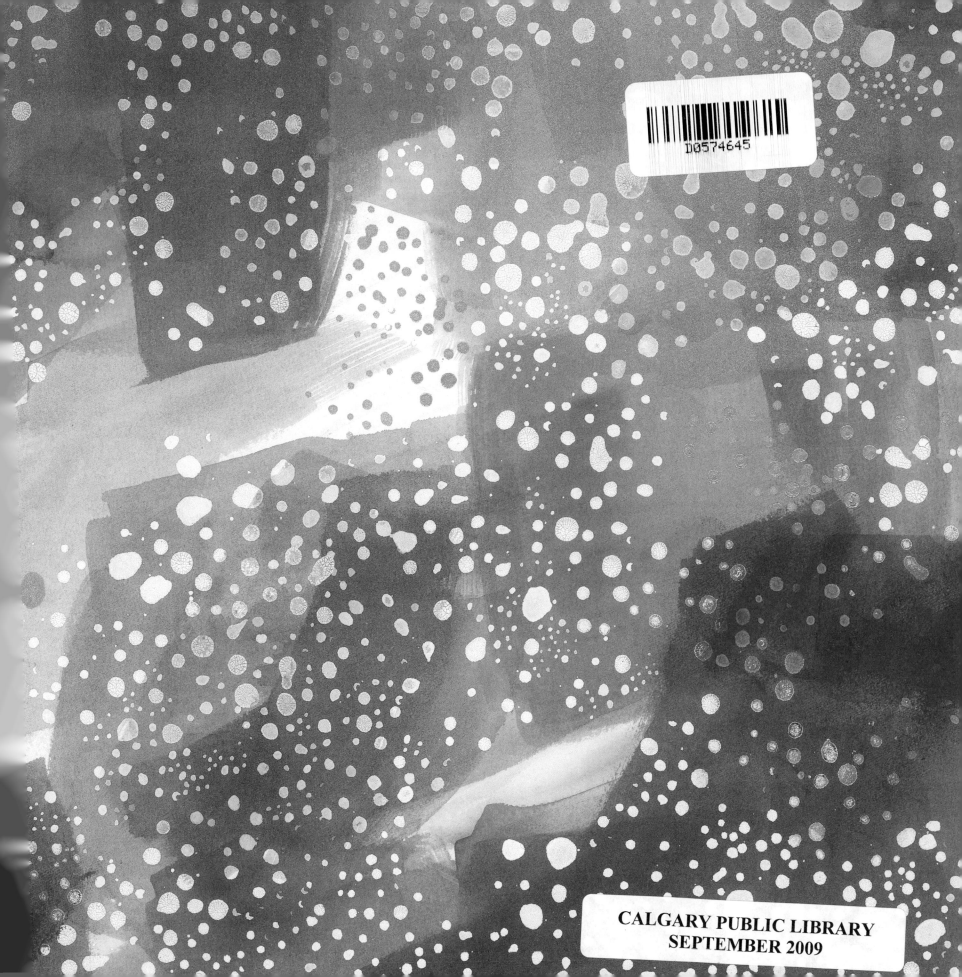

Printed in China

Text and
illustrations
copyright ©
Catherine Rayner
2009. Original edition
published in English
by Little Tiger Press,
an imprint of Magi
Publications, London,
England, 2009.
Library of Congress
Cataloging-in-Publication
Data: Rayner, Catherine.
Sylvia and Bird / Catherine
Rayner. p. cm.   Summary: Sylvia, a
dragon, overcomes her loneliness
and finds a true friend in Bird.
ISBN 978-1-56148-661-8 (hardcover :
alk. paper) [1. Dragons--Fiction.
2. Birds--Fiction. 3. Best friends--
Fiction. 4. Friendship--Fiction.
5. Loneliness--Fiction.] I. Title.
PZ7.R2297Syl 2009
[E]--dc22
2008033194

For the little ones – Jacob, Sol, Michael and Abbie ~ CR

Sylvia and Bird

Catherine Rayner

Intercourse, PA 17534
800/762-7171
www.GoodBooks.com

In a faraway place,
on a high mountaintop,
lived a shimmer-shiny
dragon named Sylvia.

Sylvia loved her leafy home,
but sometimes she felt sad.

She had searched the whole world

but never found any other dragons. Sylvia was lonely.

She gave a big,
blustery sigh.
Humfff!

And there, under the leaves,
was a small, surprised bird!

Bird was building a nest, and Sylvia thought she might be able to help.

Bird and Sylvia became friends.

Being together was so much fun.

Bird and Sylvia spent all their
days together, just like friends do.

But when Bird went to
chit-chatter with the other birds,
Sylvia felt alone.

Bird belonged with the other birds
but Sylvia was different. She had
no dragons to belong with.

Sylvia crept away. She gazed up at the night sky. Maybe there were other dragons, living on the moon? She could go and see, but the thought of leaving Bird made Sylvia feel sadder than ever.

But Bird saw that Sylvia was unhappy. She had an idea. They would go to the moon together!

Off they set, racing up through the clear blue skies!

But as Bird and Sylvia
whirled higher and higher
Bird grew cold . . .
        and tired . . .

        Suddenly she
        began to tumble . . .

        down

        down

        down through the clouds . . .

With a cry Sylvia swooped to catch her
tiny friend and gently carried her home.

And there they stayed . . .

. . . for Sylvia realized
she didn't need other dragons
to be happy. The best friend
in the world was loving,
loyal Bird.